CHRIS RIDDELL

Mr
Underbed

ANDERSEN PRESS

One night, just as Jim was dozing off,

the bedsprings CREAKED...

. . . the mattress SHOOK . . .

. . . and a head poked out from under Jim's bed.

"Hello!" it said. "I'm Mr Underbed."

"Hello," replied Jim. "I'm Jim."

"It's very uncomfortable sleeping on the floor under your bed every night. Do you mind if I join you?" asked Mr Underbed politely.

"Not at all," said Jim.

Mr Underbed fell asleep in no time, but his snoring kept Jim wide awake. Jim went to the chest of drawers to get his earmuffs . . .

. . . but when he opened the drawer, TWO heads popped up.

"Hello!" they said. "We're the top drawer twins, Crinkle and Crumple."

"Hello," answered Jim.

"You don't mind, do you?" asked Crinkle.

"Only it's very cramped in your drawer," explained Crumple, as they jumped into Jim's bed.

Crinkle and Crumple fell asleep
almost immediately, but they
pinched all the bedclothes
and Jim was too cold to
go to sleep.

So Jim went to the
wardrobe to get his
dressing-gown . . .

. . . but when he opened the wardrobe door, yet another head popped out.

"Hello!" it called. "I'm Weggie the wardrobe hound."
"Oh no!" said Jim.

"I suppose you want to sleep in my bed too?" said Jim.
"That's very kind of you," replied Weggie.

"I'm going to get to the bottom
of this," Jim muttered to himself.

Jim went right round his room opening
his toy trunk . . .

his cupboards . . .

his drawers . . .

looking behind
his curtains . . .

and under his chair . . . and out of all these places
more heads came popping up.

Tiny and Tubby Bear marched out of the cupboard.
Saggy and Squeak were under the chair.

Hooter the elephant and his friends, Swish and Sniffer,
peeped round the curtains.

And out came . . .

Bumble the middle drawer dog, Pinkie the bedside table rabbit, Grimble, Grumble and Groan the toy trunk triplets, Wid the bottom drawer mite, and last but not least little Willy Glow-nose from the lampshade.

"I give up!" said Jim.

"Everybody can sleep in my bed tonight!"

And so they did.

"Goodnight," they called

and quickly fell asleep.

Jim was quite tired after opening
all those cupboards and drawers
and so he curled up on the floor
and was soon fast asleep.

"Wake up, Jim," called his mother in the morning. "Why are you sleeping on the floor?"

"It just seemed more comfortable than my bed last night," said Jim with a smile.

ISLINGTON 6|10

Please return this item on or before the last date stamped below or you may be liable to overdue charges. To renew an item call the number, or access the online catalogue from the library webpage, details below.

1 3 DEC 2010	0 2 JUL 2012	
2 6 FEB 2011		
2 2 MAR 2011		
2 8 MAY 2011	2 3 JUL 2012	
1 2 SEP 2011		
1 3 FEB 2012		
2 1 FEB 2012		
- 3 APR 2012		

Library and Cultural Services

020 7527 6900   www.islington.gov.uk/libraries

For Klaus

Other books by
CHRIS RIDDELL
The Birthday Presents
A Little Bit of Winter
Rabbit's Wish
What Do You Remember?

First published in Great Britain in 1986 by Andersen Press Ltd.
This edition with new illustrations first published in 2009 by Andersen Press Ltd.,
20 Vauxhall Bridge Road, London SW1V 2SA.
Published in Australia by Random House Australia Pty.,
Level 3, 100 Pacific Highway, North Sydney, NSW 2060.
Copyright © Chris Riddell, 1986 and 2009.
The rights of Chris Riddell to be identified as the author and illustrator
of this work have been asserted by him in accordance with the
Copyright, Designs and Patents Act, 1988.
All rights reserved.
Colour separated in Switzerland by Photolitho AG, Zürich.
Printed and bound in Singapore by Tien Wah Press.
10 9 8 7 6 5 4 3 2 1
British Library Cataloguing in Publication Data available.
ISBN 978 1 84270 821 7